THE INVISIBLE WHITE MAN

MARSHA MCCORMICK

BALBOA.PRESS
A DIVISION OF HAY HOUSE

Balboa Press books may be ordered through booksellers or by contacting:

Balboa Press
A Division of Hay House
1663 Liberty Drive
Bloomington, IN 47403
www.balboapress.com
844-682-1282

Bible League International serves under-resourced churches worldwide, equipping them with Bibles and training so they can reach their communities with the Gospel. Our ministries include Project Philip Bible studies, Bible-based Literacy, Prison Ministry and Church Planter Training.

Print information available on the last page.

ISBN: 978-1-9822-5653-1 (sc)
ISBN: 978-1-9822-5654-8 (e)

Balboa Press rev. date: 10/09/2020

Includes a bonus chapter

How to Have a Loving and Productive Life

CONTENTS

CHAPTER ONE

MY SEARCH FOR THE INVISIBLE WHITE MAN

Hi. My name is Marsha McCormick. Throughout my life I have observed people and come to the conclusion that everyone is searching for a meaningful life of love and forgiveness. But my story, like everyone else's, includes some personal experiences that don't match up with that ideal.

Furthermore, I'm afraid this story is going to cause a lot of controversy, but my heart is heavy about this subject and I feel a great need to express it. My purpose is not to offend anyone, but from experience I know people will be offended anyway. So before you read this, I'll tell you I'm not a history major and I didn't live during slave days. Yet I'm very grateful for what people have sacrificed to make this the better world it is today, even though people will say the world is messed up. It depends on who you ask.

I am grateful to be a citizen of the United States of America. I am proud that our motto is "In God We Trust." How awesome it is that God holds the world in His hands! Unfortunately, many people refuse to believe that. This complex world is filled with so many types of people that the human brain has difficulty comprehending the ways of man. God is the only one in the universe who truly understands all human motives, thoughts, words, and actions. Since we don't understand each other, we have to take the time to learn how to respect and honor one another.

I'll start off by saying that all my life I have heard about how bad the White Man is. So, even at a young age, my quest became to find this White Man who people told me was destroying their lives. In my search, I encountered a lot of prejudice—and not just among White people. Prejudice exists in every race, and that's a fact. All you have to do is be at the wrong place at the wrong time with the wrong people, and you'll encounter hate and evil. It can happen anywhere, including your own home.

I hope my story gives you some insight about growing up in an underprivileged Black neighborhood and finding out the "world" thinks you are the scum of the earth and most people don't want you around. Don't get me wrong; there have always been other races helping the Blacks, so everyone is not like that. That's why I say we've got to stop stereotyping each other. There are many famous and successful Blacks in the world. I can't speak for them about who helped them get there, but I can say for myself that several knowledgeable people helped me to become who I am today.

Fortunately, I never had a problem with racial prejudice. I guess it's because I have always liked to grow in learning. I learned that if I don't acquire some skill in getting along with other people, it would limit my ability to get the most out of life. In other words, I would be hurting myself.

Many young people stop learning as soon as they leave home, which is tragic because there's so much more to life than that. Unfortunately, some of the things they learned while growing up just aren't true. Those who have stopped learning limit themselves in so many areas: academically, spiritually, socially, and emotionally, to name a few. Let's look at these areas in greater detail.

Academically

Getting your diploma is very important. Without a diploma you can't get a high-paying job and consequently miss out on a lot of luxuries in life. You get depressed and frustrated because the new college-educated employee working next to you has the position you wanted (with the attractive pay), and you've been there ten years! It happens over and over again because of that missing diploma. It's foolish to think you'll be given positions you don't qualify for. That's like putting the cart before the horse.

Don't blame your employer for your decision to drop out of school. You have wasted your talent and ability to grow. If you won't help yourself, no one else will either. My advice is to go back to school! It's never too late to improve your life. It's best to start at an early age. Take time out to get to know yourself. Reach for attainable goals and keep going from there. The sooner you start the better, because this keeps you focused and not so apt to get distracted from your goal. Yes, you are going to go through some setbacks and disappointments, but stay focused on your goals and your dreams. It will be worth it.

Very few of us still have the same plans we had as kids. What happened? Life happened. Still, you can "fail forward," which means refusing to give up on life just because something unpleasant or dreadful happened. Jumping to quick decisions without thinking is reckless and leads to all types of trouble, so don't make snap decisions. When you don't understand, talk to a knowledgeable person. If you're uncomfortable opening up with people, Google will give you plenty of information. If it's positive, do it, as long as you're not hurting someone else in the process.

Don't be impatient and try to make things happen right now. Sometimes you have to give yourself a breather, especially when you've got more on your plate than you can handle. Slow down and examine yourself and make decisions that will better your future. If you didn't get it right the first time, dust yourself off and start over. If that doesn't work, start over again and keep trying until you are comfortable with your life.

When you're on the outside looking in, this self-improvement process looks easy. But guess what—it's not easy for any of us! We all have to find ways to maintain our lifestyles. Even if we have a regular job, we still have to stay healthy, stay out of trouble, and keep a good reputation. Achieving all of that takes a lifetime.

Spiritually

I'm not going to push the "religion" issue because there are so many different religions, but most people subscribe to some type of religion. A connection with God gives you access to a higher power, which in turn will lead to a structured, more productive life. This is sometimes called "redemptive lift."

If you haven't realized it yet, spiritual warfare is going on, both internally and externally. Internally, you are fighting against your own carnal nature and the pride of life. Externally, you are in a battle for the survival of your soul. You can't win either one of these conflicts without God's help; the only way you can win is to fight alongside a supernatural power. My point is, you can compare religions all you want, but what it boils down to is only one person can save you—Jesus Christ! He reconciled your relationship with God by dying on the cross.

As you read this book, you will see I was in dire need of someone to save me from myself and my wicked ways. And I found salvation in Jesus. He literally saved my life and helped me get started on the path to a loving and productive life.

One very important aspect of a productive life in Jesus is reading the Bible. The reason a lot of people don't like the Bible is that it highlights their need for improvement. Ingesting the Word of God takes away your power to be selfish and instead teaches you to love unconditionally. It teaches you to be a faithful steward and give ten percent of your increase (the money you earn) to the church. It encourages you to help spread the Word of God. This kind of life is hard at first if you weren't born into it, but if you let the Spirit lead you, it gets easier. Knowing Jesus and reading His Word will bring you peace even when things are going wrong. So I advise you to get into the Word of God for yourself. If you don't understand what you're reading, join a Bible study group.

Once you get started, don't stop. I've seen too many people repent and get baptized, but then they don't read the Bible for themselves. They don't listen when the Holy Spirit tries to teach them. It's like anything else: when you stop listening, you stop learning!

It's unfortunate that when things go wrong many people start thinking God has no power or maybe He doesn't care about them. If He cares so much, why has He allowed these bad things to happen? God gave you free will; you can choose to do right or wrong. Many of the wrong things that happen are the result of your own poor choices.

For instance, let's look at slavery. God doesn't make slaves; people do. People enslave others because they want to dominate each other. So if you're wondering where evil comes from, it comes from the evil thoughts and desires you allow into your life. Evil thoughts and desires lead to evil actions. God gave you the ability to control your thoughts, but if you're having trouble in that area, I advise you to get some spiritual help. Being successful at controlling your thought life is very important in your quest for a productive life.

Socially

This is a good one, especially in our current society. Social disorders are quite common because of a disconnect with other people. Why? Too much time spent on social media or video games. Social disorders have become even more pronounced in the year 2020 with the worldwide pandemic and social distancing. Cutting yourself off from others means your thinking can get skewed.

For instance, in his article "Social Distancing Comes with Psychological Fallout" (*Science News* (3/29/20), Sujata Gupta quotes Joshua Morganstein, a disaster mental health expert: "For some people, a lack of social connectedness feels as impactful as not eating." Gupta goes on to state that many quarantined people exhibit both short- and long-term mental health problems, including stress, insomnia, anxiety, depression, emotional exhaustion, and substance abuse. That's probably only the tip of the iceberg.

The *Collins Dictionary* defines *communication* as "the imparting or exchange of information, ideas, or feelings." One of the biblical definitions of *communicate* is to be an "associate, a partaker; to participate; fellowship; to share with" (*The Complete Word Study Dictionary, New Testament*). My advice is to find at least one wise, sensible person you can communicate with. A person like this is sometimes called a "mentor," someone who teaches you not only through communication but through time spent and through life example. This type of communication is key to your growth as a productive person. So don't cheat yourself by denying the need for anyone else's input. Learn from others; ask questions; accept guidance.

Let's talk about the value of asking questions. Let's say you have to attend a Monday morning meeting at work. The room is buzzing with questions as to what the meeting is about. Then the boss walks in and everybody gets quiet. When the boss finishes talking and asks if there are any questions, maybe only one or two hands go up. These people are the smart ones—the ones who know that *asking* (that is, asking the right people) is the best way to learn and grow. At the close of that meeting everyone else is thanking the people who spoke up. People who aren't afraid to ask are usually the natural leaders in the group.

As I said, communication is important, but here's a word of advice. Don't communicate with the wrong people. Hanging around people who complain and criticize all the time won't help you; instead, it will bring you down. (I'm not talking about constructive criticism, which can help make you better.) So surround yourself with positive people who will help you. It may take a while, but don't be scared to communicate and ask—that's how you grow and become more productive.

Emotionally

Wise people will tell you not to let your emotions get in the way. The ability to control your emotions is important, because if you can't, you may do all kinds of bad things when you're upset—anywhere from throwing a fit of rage to killing someone. So don't take this issue lightly. Examine yourself and try not to respond so fast to someone who's making you angry. Try to resolve the problem, but if that doesn't work, be the bigger person and walk away.

If you can learn to control your emotions, you can become a peacemaker, which, according to Matthew 5:9, means you will be blessed, and people will recognize that you are a child of God. It takes a lot of self-discipline to control your emotions, but it will reap benefits. People will come to you when they need to talk because you are approachable. Remember someone is always watching you. People will perceive your character by your actions and words, so be careful how you react and what you say around people. If, in a moment of weakness, you lose control of your emotions, they will get the wrong impression of you.

No one is perfect; we all sometimes fail in this area. But if you do, don't be too hard on yourself. Keep trying. Bottom line: If you don't get control over your emotions, it could cost you your life.

Everyone Is Related

Let's learn how to love more and be productive members of society instead of giving our hatred and resentment free rein. Put hateful thoughts aside for a while and look at how far society has come. For instance, ask several people about their family line and you will find that we all have several races mixed in. Granted, a lot of it happened before our time, but the results of the racial mixture are still there. Is that a reason to hate the half-White baby that's in our family line? Please, people, think before you act.

Here's another thing to think about: everyone's blood, no matter what race, all runs red. It all has the same DNA source. I found an article written by Eryn Brown in the *Los Angeles Times,* "Everyone on Earth Is Related to Everyone Else, DNA Shows" (7 May 2013). Peter Ralph, a computational biologist at USC, and Graham Coop, a geneticist at UC Davis, did some extensive research into people's DNA. They learned that the DNA strands you share with each of your parents are quite long; the pieces you share with your four grandparents are only half as long; the bits you share with each of your eight great-grandparents are half again as long, and so on. Peter Ralph said the longer ago an ancestor lived, the shorter the bits of DNA are likely to be.

Eryn Brown wrote, "Out of the roughly 3 billion base pairs in the human genome, Coop and Ralph . . . calculated that these segments could reveal shared ancestry stretching back about 100 generations, or 3,000 years. . . . Going back a few thousand years, Coop and Ralph were able to show that everyone on Earth is related to everyone else."

My conclusion is this: It's impossible to find that White Man, since all families and races are mixed.

The Problematic Home Life

When you were school age, there was usually a bully throwing his or her weight around. Maybe it was the guy or girl selling drugs in the bathrooms and hallways. Why are they doing this? First, because they want money *now*; they don't want to wait until they're old enough to get a job. Second, the bully wants to dominate people because he can. Exerting his power over others makes him feel good; that is, until a bigger bully comes along and takes him down. If bullies aren't stopped, they will start to break into people's houses and steal. They become menaces to society.

Bullies are sometimes found in the home. It could be any family member who uses the authority and power he or she has to do wrong. For example, if you have a spouse who curses all the time and smokes weed in front of the kids instead of spending quality time with them, then your kids aren't going to know how to treat people when they grow up and leave home. They can wind up getting advice from people telling them the wrong thing simply because you didn't teach them.

Children need to be loved. If they don't get love at home, they will get it somewhere else, which can be bad. You see that drug dealer at school having fun in the hallways all hugged up with someone or surrounded by girls who admire him. Children may search for love on line. They might find someone without knowing they're hearing from a pedophile. The child who enjoys what the pedophile is doing has no concept of how they are being abused, even though they may feel a sense of guilty pleasure.

Children and young people don't know how to deal with these emotions, and they wind up making poor choices. They can have a lot of fun doing wrong because they never learned how to live properly. Joining the drug dealer gives them a false sense of security, and they are too immature to think about the consequences. Once they join a gang, they most likely will engage in criminal activity. Unfortunately, being involved in illegal dealings may end up cutting their life short.

I'm bringing this up because I want you to realize the damage to some of these communities happened a long time before we stepped into the world. And the damage wasn't caused by the elusive White Man. Revenge and death fill the minds of children because most often these bad things had their beginnings in the home. By the time these children reach adulthood, their chance to enjoy life has disappeared and they find themselves in an ugly place.

I don't want to end this chapter on a negative note, so I'm going to encourage you to read the bonus chapter to find out what this book is really about. "How to Have a Loving and Productive Life" will teach you things like how to establish a vibrant relationship with God, how to read the Bible, and the importance of training children from the time they are small. You can avoid all the mistakes I made by doing the things presented in the bonus chapter. And the world will become a loving and productive place for you.

CHAPTER TWO

MY DYSFUNCTIONAL CHILDHOOD

The first man I saw was beating my mother and my thought was, *I'll never want a man like that!* My dad, Danny McCormick, was dysfunctional, to say the least. I don't remember a lot of details from my childhood, but here are some incidents.

One day Daddy came home from work and went to the refrigerator only to find the water pitcher empty. Like a two-year-old, he stomped around the kitchen hollering about how disappointed he was about that, how we couldn't even do one simple thing to make his life easier. Little did he know we were laughing behind his back because it was so funny.

Another time we were making noise in the house and Daddy came stomping up the stairs. He put us in the attic and slammed the door. We heard him nailing the door shut, as if he thought it was the only way he could get some peace and quiet. He didn't know there was another way out on the other side, so we escaped by running out the other door while he was still hammering.

Once Daddy came home from work and scared us half to death by sticking a knife under the front door. I think it had something to do with us kids being home alone. Every day Mom left for work a couple hours before Daddy got home. He had lectured us about not answering the door when no adults were home. I guess he was testing the limit of our obedience. Believe me, when we saw that knife, we were way too frightened to open that door!

And the biggest crisis of all (to my childish thinking) was when Daddy told us there was no such thing as Santa Claus! He said a White Man would *never* buy us a present. Who did we think put those presents under the tree? Our daddy—that's who. I cried for days on that one because I loved Santa Claus.

These stories took place while we were living in a predominantly White neighborhood, but I had vague memories of the time we lived in the Projects. I remember people throwing bottles out of windows with glass everywhere, people found dead in apartments, people being robbed and having fights, people shooting dice. The only place for kids to play was a concrete yard with weeds growing through the cracks and junk strewn around.

Life in the Projects was a sharp contrast to the mostly White neighborhood where it was safe to leave the front and back doors open to catch a fresh-smelling breeze. We had a grassy lawn, a garden, pets, and for the first time in my life, we had White friends. There were a couple of incidents, though. One time we decided to sleep on the roof to avoid the heat. Some White men in a truck spotted us and yelled out the N word. Another time we were playing football on someone's grass and we were called the N word again. On the whole, I had a beautiful time living in that neighborhood, but, as the saying goes, all good things come to an end.

The end came when Mama finally got fed up with Daddy. She left him and took us with her back to the Black neighborhood. The first day of third grade, I had a fight for knowing how to write cursive. Three months later someone stole my mother's car, and after that someone broke into our house. As a result, we got another car and had bars installed on the house windows. We had gone from freedom to incarceration in our own home. I hated the bars but understood why they were there. With all these tragedies, that White Man had to be around somewhere. He was the go-to guy to blame everything on. But where was he exactly? I had never seen him.

By the time I was grown, I was caught in the current of chaos: sex, gangs, fights, drugs, gunshots, killings, and the list went on. Yet I somehow thought it was important to please everyone, so sometimes I would have three-man day. After all, they only wanted sex, and even paid good money for it. I joined a gang, but not to do violence; it was only for protection from people who came after us. Members of the gang taught me to keep a "spare tire," which means keep another lover on the side in case the other one stops putting out. I learned how to curse, drink, lie, mess with married men, and sleep with anyone who looked good to me—including women. With all the chaos, I had become confused and began to detest men. They couldn't care less about other people's feelings or getting to know the inner person.

No White Man taught me any of those things; it was my friends and family. As a result, I was a lying, sex-addicted, self-centered person who thought I could please anyone who came my way.

Around this time, I met my first husband. He was a big, strong, muscular guy with an education. *A great catch*, I thought. So we got married. He worked and I took care of the home, but I was a bad girl. I lied and told him my girlfriend was my stepsister. I just couldn't give her up. Needless to say, that marriage didn't last long because I found out my "good guy" husband liked to hit women. I was a lover, not a fighter, so we got a divorce. My girlfriend joined the police force and I joined the army.

CHAPTER THREE

MY DYSFUNCTIONAL ARMY LIFE

Oh boy, the things I could tell you about the army days. My sex addiction combined with a heart to please made it seem like I was in paradise. All those beautiful bodies! But how did I get to them? Fortunately, I had never been prejudiced, and I soon found out getting to them was easy. All it took was going to a club and meeting people who weren't prejudiced and there it was—sex and fun. I slept with anyone of any race, but I couldn't let the army know I was bisexual because in those days that kind of person would be dishonorably discharged. I was invited to some orgies, but it was too many people in one room for me, so of course I had to come up with another plan to get the girls.

I would drive fifty miles away from the army post to a gay club and give the girls a fake name. I thought I had the best of both worlds. Well, it worked for a while, but then the people I was dating began wanting a serious relationship, but I had no idea what that was. People were crying over me and I didn't understand. I loved people—not just one type of person—any type of person. And I thought we were just having fun.

I got pregnant by a married man. He wanted the baby; I didn't. I didn't believe in breaking up homes, so he asked me to be his mistress. There was no way I was going to be somebody's mistress, so I had an abortion, which ended the relationship.

My dates started going bad. I would make appointments, inviting several people at once, and when they showed up there would be arguments and fights. The police would be called out to my place. Women would threaten to tell on me if I broke up with them. Men would stalk me. Some people involved in the orgies were married or dating and they were breaking up with their spouses. But guess what? In all of this there was no White Man—just me and my selfishness. My life was screwed up, and I was doing it all by myself.

CHAPTER FOUR

MY FOUR-YEAR CRACK DEGREE

I got discharged from the service, got a job, and attended college, working toward a degree in the medical field. My ideal was that every patient should be treated as though they were the healthcare worker's own family—but the reality was a far cry from that ideal. I worked with physically challenged people in their homes, and saw the other caretakers were often mistreating their patients. Some were careless about things like taking vital signs, updating patient records, changing soiled sheets, and being poor patient advocates. I reported what I saw, and it backfired on me because I was the new hire.

My depression caused me to turn to drugs. I became so messed up I got kicked out of my apartment and ended up living on the street. I did this off and on for about four years, which is why I call it my "Four-Year Crack

Degree." I would befriend people I met on the street learning more about human behavior than I could handle. It was overwhelming. I listened to so many problems over those four years that it left me thirsty for the truth. Everyone had a unique set of problems, and I wanted to find out the right way to solve them.

But first I had to solve my own problems. I checked into rehab, which is where my true understanding of life started. I realized in order to get help I must tell all, and boy did I have a lot to tell! I was dumbfounded when the professionals told me I didn't understand anything about healthy relationships because I had never had one. And they added that with my sexual appetite there was no way I was going to have a normal relationship. I had always longed for a special relationship, but my hang-ups, misconceptions, and ignorance had only brought me to disaster. The only absolute truth I was able to find was in the Bible, so I started reading it every day. It didn't happen overnight, but my life started to get better. The more I read the Bible, the more my life improved.

Then along came husband number two. Even though husband number one had the advantage of an education, he was abusive and things had not ended well. So this time I thought, *Why not pick a husband with a lot less education? Maybe I'll have greater success.* Things started out well. Husband number two seemed to have many good qualities: he had a good factory job, he was good at fixing our car, he was good in bed, and he was a good cook. Best of all, he consented to go to church with me. He lacked one thing, though: he couldn't read and write.

I met husband number two at the factory where I was working as a temp. He seemed irresistible with all those great qualities. Our relationship seemed to start on its own. I was broke—only recently out of rehab. I explained to him that although he made good money at the factory, my pay grade was so low that I wouldn't be working with him much longer. Besides, I usually didn't date coworkers, but I wanted to date him, so I quit. It wasn't long before I got pregnant and had our first baby, a little girl. Tragically, she died from crib death. Our second child was a boy, and we got married. Now we needed better health insurance, so I got a job and began encouraging my husband to go back to school.

Unfortunately, I found out my husband's family often occupied themselves by standing around a barrel, drinking alcohol, and blaming all their problems on the White Man. My husband seemed to agree with them. He told me it was the White Man's fault that he hadn't got an education. I thought, *Here we go again.* I told him that wasn't true and helped him enroll in a free school so he could earn a GED, equivalent to a high school diploma. But he dropped out and things went sour. I asked him, "Where is that White Man who is holding you back?" He just looked at me funny as he guzzled his beer, so I pointed to the bottle: "*There* is that White Man! That beer you can't quit drinking! Did a White Man come to that school and make you quit, or did you quit on your own?" I was upset, but I didn't want another divorce so I tried hard to understand him.

He stopped going to church with me, drank more, stopped paying bills, and his performance in bed went down due to excessive drinking. I asked him, "What happened to you?" He said, "You make enough money to pay all the bills, so I shouldn't have to give you any money. I can do whatever I want."

During the nine years we were together, I also quit going to church. We got divorced. I got to thinking about the years I had wasted on him and all the women I had passed up. I went ape nuts, dating five women in one weekend. As I lay there after it was over, the Holy Spirit came and convicted me so strongly that I promised God I would not stop going to church no matter what happened, and I would date only one person at a time. Still, I couldn't make myself give up women because it seemed like they were better to me than any man had ever been. Yet when I tried having a long-term relationship with a woman, I found out she treated me no better than any man had.

I didn't understand why certain people in the world were so angry and evil about everything. Furthermore, I didn't see a difference in any race, except for the skin color. It became quite clear to me: no White Man had screwed up my life; I had nobody to blame but myself.

After several years of floundering around in that perverse environment, I had an intense hunger to learn to do right. I had a five-year-old son to think about. I stopped dating for a while and continued attending Black churches. One day I asked the leadership for counseling, and one of the deacons came over to my house and tried to initiate sex with me. He was a married man and I wanted no part of that! Besides, I was tired of them passing around the offering basket three to five times a service, so I decided to find another church.

Tired of the constant talk about the evil White Man, I found a multicultural church and felt the Spirit as soon as I entered the door. They welcomed and accepted me for who I was, which was a new experience. For the last few years, I had been a UPS driver. At my former church, I had once come in dressed in my uniform because I had just got off work and didn't want to miss church. Just about everyone in that church wore dresses and suits, and they looked at me like I had committed a sin. I just wanted to go to church in peace, but they made me feel uncomfortable. At this new church there was no censure, no pressure to give extra money, no harassment about dressing a certain way, and the services were excellent.

CHAPTER FIVE

YOUR CHILDREN, YOUR FUTURE VALUE THEM ENOUGH TO BE A GOOD EXAMPLE

Now that you have a sense of who I am, let's get to the heart of this story. First of all, if we as parents claim to love our children, we must let them see that we are living by a moral compass. Our children are our future, and we need to prepare them for a good life by being good examples in front of them. We can't blame the White Man for our children turning out bad if all they've seen in their life is divorce, drugs, alcoholism, anger issues, and joblessness. Most likely they will grow up with the same attitude and habits. It's called the generational curse.

I will concede that Blacks are under the gun because some people consider us the scum of the earth. That's a shame, because most Blacks are good people. Truth be told, you can find scum in every race, so why is it so often attributed just to Blacks? For instance, take the news media. They seem to report on Black crimes more than the crimes of any other race. I have to admit that until I watched true-crime shows on television, I had no idea that criminals came in all genders, sizes, ages, and races. I'm not trying to let Blacks off the hook, but we certainly aren't doing ourselves any favors when we are featured on live television for looting, rioting, and destroying our own neighborhoods. We must learn to control our anger and represent ourselves better. We must be mindful of what we do because our children will be watching those news reports in the future.

By the time kids leave home, most of them have seen a lot—too much in fact. There are a fortunate few who haven't had very many bad experiences, but they too sometimes decide to do illegal things, out of boredom, I guess. Let me tell you this: Doing bad things is like spewing ugly words out of your mouth and then trying to put them back, which is impossible. Likewise, once you do something illegal, it is out there forever, even if you have enough money to cover it up legally. Most people will know you paid your way out of trouble, which tarnishes your reputation for life. It's just not worth it.

I had to go to rehab to figure out what was going on in my life because my parents didn't teach me when I was young. How could I be expected to tell the difference between right and wrong when they had not lived good lives before me and taught me how to do right? On the other hand, there are parents who have lived exemplary lives in front of their children, and the kids still go wrong. But at least those parents know they have given their children enough tools to make a good decision, even if they ended up making a bad one.

All of us need to understand that what we do and say in front of our children will affect them for the rest of their lives. We can either raise them in a nurturing environment and teach them good principles to live by, or we can raise them in a dysfunctional, drugged-up, abusive environment that will inflict pain and confusion for the rest of their lives. We can't expect our children to treat others with love and respect when they see us treating others (including them) with hatred, disrespect, and abuse. The characters of children are formed at home before the age of six, and most of those poor children miss the first steps to a loving and productive future. Some children have to endure so much evil in the eighteen years they are under their parents' control that by the time they get out on their own they're unfit for society.

Unfortunately, the children are the ones who suffer the most from our bad choices. They are like blank tapes, and we, as parents, are responsible for recording either good or bad things on those tapes. Bad recordings are nearly impossible to erase, which means our behaviors and words will remain in our kids' heads for the rest of their lives, even after we are gone. Some poor children suffer simply because they witnessed the grownups in their lives doing all kinds of despicable things behind closed doors. Then those same grownups put on a public face that gives the impression they are nice and kind, when inside they are miserable and evil. They go home and say all kinds of ungodly things in front of their children. I have heard of people who even have sex in front of their children, or worse, have sexual relations *with* their children. Just thinking about tragedies like these hurts my heart and turns my stomach.

Teach your children how to communicate effectively so they can get where they need to go in society. Instill principles of right and wrong in their lives. Live a moral life in front of them. Have enough love and compassion to realize it is your responsibility to be a moral compass for your children so they won't go out into the world with bitterness, confusion, hatred, and anger. None of that will help them; it will only hurt them—if not get them killed. It's hard to be productive when someone has crammed your head with a bunch of garbage. Getting along with others and being respectful is the answer for your children to go in the right direction to reach their full potential. You'll find people of all races who are willing to help others when they are respectful.

Most parents want their children to be happy and have successful relationships, but how can you expect them to forge good relationships when you've taught them nothing about wise dating practices? If they haven't been taught values in the home, they won't know how to conduct themselves, how to choose good friends, or how to communicate with people. Most likely, they will get "used." Children and young people are vulnerable if you haven't taught them and covered them with prayer. Too many children, both boys and girls, have gone missing or have been taken by pedophiles or sex traffickers. I know this is hard to talk about with your children, but that's just what the predator wants you to do—tell your children nothing and leave them vulnerable. If you don't warn your children about potential dangers, it makes the predator's job easier to persuade your innocent child to do wrong. Your children may gripe about your constant communication with them, but they are getting the message—*Mom and Dad care about me.*

Start early in teaching your children about dating. Preteens aren't too young to be given guidelines on choosing the right friends and setting safe boundaries for what they will and won't do. When they are old enough to date, talk to your children before they leave the house. They will go out of the home knowing that you love them, and they will not want to disappoint you. Preparing them ahead of time for the dating game will save them a lot of grief later on. (See chapter six for more teaching about dating.)

Parents, pay close attention to your children and you will be more apt to pick up on signals that something is wrong, like when they tell you they don't want to be left alone with the babysitter or they act a little strange after coming home from school. Build a good relationship with your children so they are comfortable talking to you about anything. Some parents think it's enough to just clothe and feed their children, but that's not enough. They need your time, your attention, your good advice, and your love.

Don't let someone you don't know train your child; you don't know what kind of garbage they will put in your child's head. Be up front with your children and tell them the truth. For instance, some children may come home with an attitude after spending time at a friend's house, complaining that their friend has video games or expensive sneakers or a nice allowance or maybe their parents gave them a car. You have to explain to them that every household is different. Some people have more; some people have less. Be on the lookout for teachable moments like these. You don't want to lose your child because of something like jealousy or envy.

Take the blinders off and get a good look at the true situation. You are a life coach to your children—not their forever owner. You have only so many years to instill integrity, goodness, respectability, and productivity in them.

CHAPTER SIX

THE DATING GAME PLAY BY THE RIGHT RULES

There are rules for almost any game. In order to win fair and square, you (any everyone else playing the game) have to follow the rules. Anyone who wins by cheating may gloat over their triumph, but inside they feel no satisfaction or sense of accomplishment. That's because cheating robs a person of his or her integrity. And if they will cheat at one game, they will cheat at any other game too.

Did you know there are rules for playing the dating game? Some of these rules are set by social norms (society's idea of correct behavior). Some rules are set by parents in order to protect their teenagers from getting hurt. But what happens if the social norms don't match up with God's rules? What happens if the parents don't care what their teenagers do as long as their own lives aren't interrupted by their kids getting arrested or having illegitimate grandchildren or running off? So, although the dating game doesn't directly pertain to my search for the invisible White Man, I think this subject is an important one to talk about.

The dating game can be treacherous because so many people aren't playing by the right rules. It's dangerous to believe everything they say because many of them are such good liars. The wise thing to do is take the time to *wait* and *investigate.* Don't get so tangled up in your desires in the heat of the moment that you pass up all the red flags without stopping. Before you know it, you are stuck on a feeling, not of love but of lust. That lustful feeling can lead you into all kinds of dangerous behaviors, including stalking, domination, fights, addictions, and in some cases, murder. It's not worth it. I know, because I found out the hard way.

That's why I say God's rules are the most important and the safest rules by which to play the dating game. Anyone who follows those rules has a wonderful sense of satisfaction and accomplishment when they win. Let's look a little deeper into this important subject.

First of all, the Bible doesn't specifically address dating; however, it does contain biblical principles that can be applied to dating. In biblical times, the engagement period was called a betrothal. According to *Easton's Bible Dictionary*, the betrothal usually took place a year or more before marriage and involved a contract with a specific time when the couple would get married. From the time of betrothal, the woman was regarded as the lawful wife of the man to whom she was betrothed. From this example we can conclude that dating is not as casual a matter as the world would have us think.

Here are a just a few things I have learned regarding Christian dating:

Self-control is a must in every part of a Christian's life. Once you learn to control yourself—your thoughts, your desires, your actions—then you will be eligible to play the dating game. Here are some guidelines God has set for dating:

1. The apostle Paul said in 1 Cor. 3:16–17, if you are a Christian, then your body is a holy temple.
2. He warned, "If someone destroys God's temple, God will destroy him. For God's temple is holy, which is what you are" (1 Cor. 3:16–17, NET). It is vital to keep your temple clean.
3. Paul wrote, "Therefore, since we have these promises, dear friends, let us purify ourselves from everything that contaminates body and spirit, perfecting holiness out of reverence for God (1 Cor. 7:1, NIV).
4. The apostle Peter wrote, "Like the Holy One who called you, become holy yourselves in all

> your conduct, for it is written, 'You shall be holy, because I am holy" (1 Pet. 1:15–16, NET).

You might ask, "When the Bible says we should keep our temple free of contamination, what does that mean exactly?" Well, that's a very broad subject, but when applied to dating, it involves abstinence (there's that self-control again), which is a must for a Christian who is dating.

One dictionary definition of *abstinence* is refusing to give in to a craving for intoxicating beverages or certain foods. But, according to Merriam-Webster, *abstinence* is most often associated with refraining from sexual intercourse. It goes without saying that adultery and fornication fall into the category of things a Christian should avoid while playing the dating game.

Just to be clear, *fornication* is consensual intercourse between two persons who aren't married to each other. *Adultery* is consensual intercourse between a married man and someone other than his wife or between a married woman and someone other than her husband. God's rules say to avoid both of these sexual perversions. If you follow those two rules, in the long run you'll save yourself a lot of grief.

What does the Bible say about fornication?

1. Rom. 1:29—Sexual perversion (including fornication) opens the door for all manner of sin

in your life: greed, hate, envy, murder, quarreling, deception, malicious behavior, and gossip.

2. 1 Cor. 5:1—Paul wrote, "I can hardly believe the report about the sexual immorality going on among you—something that even pagans don't do!" He was appalled that a man in the Corinthian church was sleeping with his stepmother and said they should be "mourning in sorrow and shame. And you should remove this man from your fellowship."
3. 1 Cor. 6: 18—Paul said, "Run from sexual sin! No other sin so clearly affects the body as this one does. For sexual immorality is a sin against your own body."
4. Jude 7—Sodom and Gomorrah, two wicked cities in Abraham's time, were filled with fornication and every other kind of sexual perversion. Jude warned, "Those cities were destroyed by fire and serve as a warning of the eternal fire of God's judgment."

If you're a Christian, keep your Christian standards. Stop doing what other people want you to do. Be truthful to yourself and everyone else. Be faithful at all times. Don't let any relationship obscure your faith in Christ. The right person will share your sincerity and faith in Christ. Be open to a friendship developing into something bigger, but be realistic and honest about your intentions. Make a list of points that are essential and that can be shared with each other. Stick to the moral rules. Stand firm and avoid temptation to be physical. Stay true to your values. Establish limits. Be guided by true love and pray about it. Guard your heart, because everything in your life, including physical and spiritual desires, flows from the heart.

If you want to get married and if you have settled in your mind to play by God's rules, by all means, start dating. But it's best not to date someone whom you would never consider marrying. That would be like going to the grocery store with no money; you would either leave unsatisfied or you would take something home that's not yours.

Make sure the person you are dating is unmarried. Let's look at the biblical warnings against adultery.

1. Deut. 5:18—"You shall not commit adultery." Almost everyone knows that is the seventh commandment, one of the top ten rules to follow.
2. Matt. 5:28—"Anyone who looks at a woman lustfully has already committed adultery with her in his heart." Who knew you could commit adultery just by looking? God will give you a spouse to enjoy. He will seal the union in His name. Keep your sexual activities in the home with your spouse as God intended.

3. Gal. 5:19–21—Adultery (as well as fornication) is a work of the flesh. God hates it as much as He hates the other works of the flesh listed in Galatians 5. Paul wrote, "Let me tell you again, as I have before, that anyone living that sort of life will not inherit the Kingdom of God."

Let's move to another sensitive area: alternative lifestyles. I'm the last one to look down on people who choose an alternative lifestyle because I was once in that situation. What people may not realize, however, is that society, family, and our educational system are guilty for a lot of this happening. Why? Because they exert constant pressure on kids and young people about what a man or woman is supposed to act like, look like, and how they are supposed to dress. Kids get so confused. I know, because it drove me crazy too. I eventually found out that the only person we should want to look like is Jesus. He made us, male and female, and hardwired these gender recognitions into our brains.

After you become a Christian, you are supposed to fight your sin nature with the help of the Holy Spirit and do what's right in God's eyes. In a sense, you are responsible for placing yourself in heaven or hell, according to your obedience (or disobedience) to God's Word. I'm nowhere near perfect and never will be. I'm just saying now would be a good time to examine yourself and consider a change, because we all have something to feel guilty about. God never intended for us to throw off all restraint and let our flesh dictate our actions. But I know that temptation is real and the human heart is very deceitful. In Jeremiah 17:9, the prophet stepped beyond that when he said the human heart is desperately wicked! So don't go by what you feel in your heart in the heat of the moment. Go by the principles in God's Word!

CHAPTER SEVEN

GOOD PEOPLE, BAD PEOPLE SOMETIMES IT'S HARD TO TELL THE DIFFERENCE

Let's talk about "Good People." Just to be clear, I'm referring to people of all races who are interested in no one but themselves, yet they classify themselves as "good." They may at first seem pleasant to be around, but after a while they start to stink.

You will find "Good People" on every level who think if a person doesn't think or act just like them, then they are failures. Good People think they have it all figured out, and no one can tell them any different. Guess what, Good People. There are many levels of people from rich to poor, and one level is not going to understand the people at the other levels. That doesn't mean everyone on a different level than you is bad.

If you think the whole world revolves around you, you are sadly mistaken. For instance, have you stopped to consider what people go through on a daily basis just trying to do their jobs? I'm talking about judges, lawyers, police, social workers, counselors, businessmen, teachers, pastors, and other professions that are out there serving the community and keeping it together. No, you probably haven't considered them, because it's all about you. That kind of bad attitude affects everyone around you. You only talk to people when you want something from them. Get a life. You're missing so many beautiful things by acting that way. No one is exempt from problems, so don't be so mean.

If you're so good, can you at least let someone who needs your help text you since you don't want to be bothered by a lengthy conversation? Helping somebody will not hurt you; as a matter of fact, helping others will help you—it will give you a healthier perspective on life.

Regarding the subject of not wanting to help others, I'm not talking about toxic people who deserve to be taken out of your life. For instance, a woman named Carey and I had been friends since our teenage years. We did everything together. After a while, I began noticing that if I suggested helping someone, she suddenly wanted to go home. She was "good" as long as we were having fun going to a club, especially since most of the time I was buying. Carey was a dropout, so I kept encouraging her to go back to school. I even tried to find her a job, but she would refuse and say, "I'm good." Sometimes when her phone rang, she wouldn't answer. "Why aren't you taking that call?" I would ask. She would reply, "Oh, it's just somebody wanting me to do something for them and I don't have time." I finally realized that Carey was interested only if there was something in it for her. She blocked anything out of her life that would improve her character. After twenty years of this, I found out through another friend of mine that Carey said she was just using me for whatever she could get—a ride to the store, free drinks at the club, a loan here and there. I was hurt. I didn't understand how she could be so self-centered and mercenary about our friendship. So I let her go.

They say love is blind, and I sure was blind on that one. My efforts to help Carey were only enabling her lifestyle and behavior. If you are a lender, make sure you examine yourself and the situation the borrower is in, because, if it's happening over and over, the borrower is only using you for what they can get out of you. They don't really care about you. They will take your money and spend it hanging out with their useless friends. They want whatever they can get out of you, but when it's their time to give, they want something in return. That's not "good"; that's horrible!

A genuinely Good Person gives from the heart without expecting anything in return. The Lord Jesus experienced hurt, rejection, and betrayal from His "enemies," people who were hostile to Him because His goodness convicted them. Jesus said if they hated Him, they will hate you too, because you are His child. It is comforting to know that when you're good to those who despise you, Jesus has a special promise for you: "Love your enemies, do good, and lend expecting nothing in return. If you do, you will have a great reward. You will be acting the way children of the Most High act, for he is kind to ungrateful and wicked people" (Luke 6:35, CEB). They won't give you anything in return, but Jesus will make it up to you.

Bad People can be found at every level of life—the controlling, possessive, abusive people who treat human souls like they're there for the taking. Innocent ones, beware of predators who prey on people weaker than themselves. They lie in wait like dogs and force their life on you. At one time they may have known what they're doing is wrong, but now they don't care. They have burned through their conscience so many times that it's charred beyond recognition.

Bad friends are a curse. Experience has taught me there are two types of bad friends: the fakes who pretend to be your friend but don't think twice about slandering you behind your back, and the "friends" that entice you to sin and pull you down the wrong path.

1. Psa. 140:1–3 (NLT): David prayed, "O LORD, rescue me from evil people. Protect me from those who are violent, those who plot evil in their hearts and stir up trouble all day long. Their tongues sting like a snake; the venom of a viper drips from their lips."
2. Prov. 26:24–26 (NLT): "People may cover their hatred with pleasant words, but they're deceiving you. They pretend to be kind, but don't believe them. Their hearts are full of many evils. While their hatred may be concealed by trickery, their wrongdoing will be exposed in public."
3. 1 Cor. 5:11 (NLT): "You are not to associate with anyone who claims to be a believer yet indulges in sexual sin, or is greedy, or worships idols, or is abusive, or is a drunkard, or cheats people. Don't even eat with such people."
4. 1 Cor. 15:33–34 (NLT): "Don't be fooled . . . for bad company corrupts good character. Think carefully about what is right, and stop sinning."

Real friends will teach each other how to grow in love and do better. They are genuinely Good People. What does the Bible say about them?

1. Prov. 19:17 (NLT): "If you help the poor, you are lending to the LORD—and he will repay you!"

2. Acts 20:35 (NLT): Paul told the Ephesian Christians, "I have been a constant example of how you can help those in need by working hard. You should remember the words of the Lord Jesus: 'It is more blessed to give than to receive.'"
3. Gal. 6:2 (NLT): Paul wrote to the Galtian Christians, "Share each other's burdens, and in this way obey the law of Christ."
4. Phil. 2:4 (NLT): He wrote to the Philippian Christians, "Don't look out only for your own interests, but take an interest in others, too.
5. Heb. 13:16 (NLT): "Don't forget to do good and to share with those in need. These are the sacrifices that please God."

Bad People versus Good People

1. Psa. 1:1–4 (ERV) says, "Great blessings belong to those who don't listen to evil advice, who don't live like sinners, and who don't join those who make fun of God. Instead, they love the Lord's teachings and think about them day and night. So they grow strong, like a tree planted by a stream—a tree that produces fruit when it should and has leaves that never fall. Everything they do is successful. But the wicked are not like that. They are like chaff that the wind blows away.

2. Matt. 7:12 (NLT) says, "'Do to others whatever you would like them to do to you.' This is the essence of all that is taught in the law and the prophets."

As you can see, "Bad People versus Good People" is not a Black-and-White issue; *it is a character issue.*

CHAPTER EIGHT

CONCLUSION: THIS IS NOT A BLACK-AND-WHITE WORLD IT IS GOD'S WORLD

At last, my quest for finding the invisible White Man is over. My conclusion is that no one will ever find him. Why? Because he's not there. Every person I thought was White would say,

"I'm not White, I'm Italian" (or Irish or German or Latino or Mexican or Indian or Russian or Chinese or Jewish, and the list goes on). I think the media is to blame for much of the agitation over prejudice, because that's all the people hear on the news. The only way to stop the agitation is to get the media to report the news without bias so that the world won't think it's just the Blacks doing wrong most of the time. People of all races can do right or wrong.

Property values go down when Blacks move into the neighborhood. Is that because of prejudice? No. It's because of the way we disrespect our own people and our property. No one wants their community to be destroyed because of you and your bad choices and bad attitude. The way our property looks is the first impression people get. You can tell when you're coming to most Black neighborhoods because there's trash all over, vacant buildings, busted windows, doors kicked in, and copper and fixtures have been torn out. Who's going to buy the building after it's wrecked? Who's going to keep fixing the damage only to have to fix it all over again? Even I have a hard time understanding that. If your yard is trashy, clean pick it up. Leave the vacant buildings alone. I understand your pain, but I don't understand why you act out your feelings in that way. It's unacceptable! We, as Black people, have to do better! We need to stop blaming the White Man for all of our problems and take a good look at how we represent ourselves.

As I drive through some neighborhoods, I just want to cry because of things I see people doing. I see them standing at the bus stop cursing and smoking weed. They're shooting guns at night and keeping their own people oppressed because they can't enjoy watching the sun go down with fear of being shot in the dark. It's disrespectful and disgraceful. How can you expect someone to respect you when they see you doing things like that? No one is going to think well of you when you're showing disrespect.

The Importance of Well-Chosen Words

We all speak different "languages" within our language. For example, if I walk up to a lady and say, "How you doin', Old G?" she may take it as an insult because she doesn't know me. To me the term means "the lady in charge." In my "language," it's somewhat of an honor to be called Old G. But to her it might mean Old Gal, Old Bag, or Old Ogre. We both speak English, but she doesn't understand my language.

There's a lot of misunderstanding because of the words we choose when talking to people, so take the time to ask more questions, especially if the other person says something that offends you. They may not have said it to you if they knew it meant something different to you.

All conversations are important, and we don't know what's going to come out of them. What a lot of people don't realize is every time we open our mouth, our character is on the line. We are especially sensitive when talking to a person from a different race. Even though we weren't the ones who did or said something wrong, we're going to be judged by the people in that other race. So think hard when speaking with someone from a different race because, whether you know it or not, you represent your people. That may not be fair, but it's true.

Most important, you represent *you*. How do you want people to think of you? Some people don't care how they represent themselves, which is a shame because the beauty inside of them won't get exposed because of the ugliness they show on the outside. God designed them better than that, but they keep choosing to do wrong. For instance, you can go to the store and see someone screaming and cursing at a clerk with a store full of people looking on. That's so disrespectful and it ruins your character. That clerk is there to serve you and she doesn't deserve treatment like that. Not only do you ruin the clerk's day, you ruin the days of the people behind you in line.

We've Got to Do Better

Let's stop the finger-pointing and blaming everyone else for our problems. For one thing, we're only hurting ourselves by killing each other, and killing the police when they're trying to bring law and order to our lives and our neighborhoods. We've got to love our neighbors instead of robbing our neighbors. We've got to respect the business people in our neighborhoods who are trying to serve the community. It isn't right to hurt others, especially our own kind! The only thing I can say to people who are out there rioting all day and night is . . .

- Quit allowing yourselves to be influenced by the lies of politicians and the media.
- Quit overreacting to every event before you even know the facts about what happened.
- Quit all of this destruction and rioting and do something useful!

You think you are making the world a better place, but you're not. You're destroying it as well as your chance to have a good life.

We can't expect people to understand us when we're living destructive, nonproductive lives. I say it's high time we start doing our part—pulling our own weight. We should be picking up trash, not throwing it around. We should be making our yards look good instead of filling them up with junk and letting the weeds take over. We should stop breaking windows and burning vacant buildings; it just drags down the property values in our communities. Some of these protests are horrible and violent. We're tearing up our own communities. And guess who is there to clean up the mess and repair the damage? Mostly the White people, the very ones who you say are out to get you.

We've Got to Stop Disrespecting Our Community Environment

I love people so much that dealing with wrongdoing every day drives me insane. I hate the fact that people are so inconsiderate by throwing paper and trash and garbage all over the ground with no concern for the earth and people who have to pick up behind them. That one crime of littering affects the streets. It makes the environment look so bleak and tasteless. When I see a lot of trash littering the streets, my heart just sinks with grief. Littering also affects ocean life. How many of you are willing to admit that? It is not right and it is damaging our streets and oceans. Let's have some compassion for the earth pick up our trash.

Let's stop talking hatred and start talk healing. Let's root up the evil and plant some good seeds. Get a job, even if it's temporary. Cut grass or shovel snow. Do odd jobs. Be productive. You'll feel better about yourself, and the world will be a better place.

I know some people who started their own lawn business. They got so many customers that they had to hire other friends to help them, and ended up being successful. They stopped doing their bad habits. You never know what can happen unless you try. As they say, "Nothing beats a failure but a try."

It's Not the Dope Man's Fault

You've got to stop blaming the dope man for your problems; you're the one who's buying the dope. People who fall into the dope trap are only destroying their health and scrambling their brains. If you use drugs and find yourself not being able to function (meaning not able to work or do your obligations), you should just stop because you are not strong enough for it. You need to stop doing bad things like stealing and hawking stolen goods to get your dope.

I pray that it will all go away, but that won't happen because people are freewill agents; they can choose to do whatever they want. I just wish the people that are going too far would turn to a counselor and talk about what they're doing to themselves. But drugs dealers aren't going to go away, so if we can't beat them, let's find other ways to get rid of our scum-of-the-earth reputation without the violence. We can't get rid of all of it because we're always going to have people who think they can rob the dope man or not give him the money they owe and the shooting starts. It happens other places than black neighborhoods too, only the media doesn't report it.

Let People See Your Beauty

What does that mean: "Let people see your beauty"? I'm not talking about outward beauty, which is only skin deep. What really counts is inner beauty. My question for you is, "How can anyone see your beauty when all you show them is hate and ugly actions?"

I submit that we need to look at people for their character, not their skin color or looks. For instance, some of those White people we blame everything on even joined the peaceful protest marches. We all need to work on ourselves and find a moral compass to keep us accountable for our actions.

You may have heard the slogan from the 1960s, "Black Is Beautiful." Well, about twenty years later, a black child came home from school upset because one of his classmates had taunted him in front of the whole class about his curly hair and dark skin. When he got home, he told his mama, craving her comfort and expecting she would threaten to confront the mean boy. Instead, she went into the bedroom, came back with a slip of paper, and told her child to memorize what was on that paper. That night when he looked at the paper, he recognized his grandma's handwriting. The words said,

> The Black Is Beautiful Recipe
>
> 1 cup pride
> 2 cups confidence
> 4 "I don't cares" [what other people say or think of me]

2 fierce comebacks [sometimes it's hard to turn the other cheek]
1 teaspoon of strut your stuff
3 teaspoons of love
3 cups of inner peace
2–1/2 teaspoons sweetness

Instructions: Cream together the pride and confidence until the mixture is light, fluffy, and you can feel the goodness deep within your soul. Add the "I don't cares" one at a time, being sure that each one is fully incorporated and that you truly mean it.

When the child was grown, he wrote about this memory: "That night, as I looked over my grandmother's neat handwriting, I realized that I had nothing to worry about. My hair, skin, and full features didn't need to be validated by some snotty nosed kid in my class. The only opinion that mattered was my own."

Let that sink in: the only opinion that really matters is your own. How can you have a high opinion of yourself when all you feel is prejudice and hate and violence? Your conscience has been burned so many times that it's too weak to prod you when you do something wrong. Please understand that evil sends you backward, not forward. You'll never be able to respect yourself until you start doing better. You'll never be beautiful outside until you're beautiful inside.

I'm sorry if my words offend you, but it's the truth. In all my life experiences, I found only one real truth—the Bible. As I learned to study the Bible, I found so many valuable stories and teachable moments that it blew my mind. I found out the best way to get the whole effect was to read it from beginning to end. The more I learned from reading His Word, the more I realized I needed to learn. For one thing, I learned God is sensitive about how a person approaches Him, so make sure you do it with a humble spirit. I found that God gives me what I need to do the job He has assigned to me. (Like writing this book, for example.)

The Pandemic and the State of Our Country

Why are we so blind that we can't see this pandemic that crippled the whole world is God's warning of what is to come? You think this pandemic is bad, just keep on living. Look in the Bible to find out what the future holds. For many, their pride has blinded their eyes to the truth. Instead of pointing fingers at each other, we ought to be fasting and praying for God to stop this pandemic—because we sure can't.

A lot of us are ignoring the Creator by looking for man to solve the pandemic problem. Think about it:

who is powerful enough to do such a thing? Don't get me wrong; I'm not saying we don't need to try to figure out what to do. It is good that the medical field is doing everything they can to produce a vaccine. I think it's good that we come together and make the best decisions we know how to make to keep us safe. But to blame a few people, or the President, for example, for the actions of each individual is not right. Everyone should do their part and wear a mask, but rebellion in the heart of man makes it impossible to control everyone.

The United States has been established only 244 years and was rooted "In God We Trust," but now we want to throw God away and do things our way. We only turn to God when we are in trouble. We've taken Him out of so many places now that the United States looks like Sodom and Gomorrah. I pray that the world will learn to honor their Creator, but I know my prayer will not be answered until Jesus comes. I'm here to tell you God wins in the end. We need to come together as a whole and learn how to respect and love one another and do something productive. We should stop blaming the White Man and others for our failures. We should let our resentment go and move forward.

History has shown us that we need each other. For those of you who say we don't, what happens when someone gets stranded on an island or lost while hiking or caught in a housefire or a child goes missing? You are right in thinking, "Well, eventually those people will be found and rescued because there are loving and productive people standing by every day willing to risk their own lives to save someone else." That's why I say claiming you don't need anyone could be dangerous.

For example, I read a story one time about these two brothers who very rarely went outside of their large, rambling old house. They stayed in there for years until the roof rotted and their water and electricity were turned off. They accumulated tons of junk—old pianos, newspapers and magazines, kitchen appliances, furniture, gadgets and gizmos, you name it—and set booby traps because they were scared someone was going to come in and try to steal their stuff. Eventually, one of the brothers died because he got sick and didn't get medical care. The other one died when he got caught in one of his own booby traps and lay there until he starved to death because no one knew he needed help. The authorities didn't find the two brothers until several weeks later when neighbors started complaining because of the smell. Those brothers took the "I don't need anyone" attitude to the extreme and paid for it with their lives.

Realize the importance of everyone doing their part. You may be asking, "What's that got to do with me? I'm only one person. Anything I do won't make any difference." I'm telling you it will. In every walk of life, people want to be respected and loved, including you. The only way you yourself can feel respected and loved is to show the same to others. Mutual respect and treating others how you would like to be treated is the best way to have a sound mind and clear conscience. When your conscience is doing its job (telling you that you did something wrong), it will prod you when you hurt someone, even if it is accidently. That feeling of guilt hits you, and if you don't make it right, that mistake will become part of your character. So make sure you fix those mistakes immediately.

In contrast, some people have overridden the prodding of their conscience so many times that the poor little guy gives up and dies. People like that don't care what they do or who they do it to. They want what they want when they want it, and they don't think about the consequences because they don't care. Don't waste your time trying to figure them out or fix them by trying to talk to them about their actions and attitudes because they probably won't respond. You are just trying to help, but they don't want you butting in. In the end, you'll be the one who gets hurt.

People with damaged consciences don't care how their behavior affects others. People who run red lights, whiz through stop signs, trail the bumper of your car, or vent their road rage are violating the law. This behavior causes all kinds of bad accidents from minor to fatalities. Then there are people who go to the doctor and get impatient about the wait. They're rude to the doctor's assistant. They talk so loud and disrespectfully in the waiting room that it ruins your day—and probably everyone else's too. Some people will go to the gas station and drive away without paying for their gas. Or they will steal something off the shelves in the store. Some will jump ahead of you in line at the grocery store or even bump you from behind with their grocery cart. All these instances can escalate from minor altercations to major incidents and the police have to be called. People of all races exhibit these behaviors, and they are being bad examples. We need to learn as a whole not to be so quick to tear people down. Let's have some mercy. Let's be patient. Let's be kind.

Speaking of the police, they are there to protect us and to deal with lawbreakers. Killings, break-ins, accidents, robberies, the list goes on. I don't understand why people want jobs in law enforcement because they aren't paid enough to offset the people who hate them and resent them when they try to do their job. Some people resist arrest or even lure police into staged situations just so they can hurt them. But stop for a minute to imagine what the world would be like without law enforcement. The sin nature in people would take over. The strong would constantly be taking advantage of the weak. Criminals would go berserk because there would be no restraint and no consequences. There would be anarchy, chaos, rioting, hijacking, pirating, and murder.

The reason I am talking about this reality is because some people think we don't need law enforcement. They think the world would be a better place without it. I'm here to tell you the world would *not* be a better place. For example, you might be the one getting robbed, mugged, your identity stolen, your car stolen, your house burned down, your home invaded. And there would be no 911 to call for help. We would become a third-world country. I'm writing this to say I'm grateful for law enforcement. I personally don't think they get enough money for that job.

This Is God's World

In the end, this is not the White Man's world or the Black Man's world; it is God's World. Yet the wiser we get in our own eyes, the more we think we are the ones ruling the world. We have taken God's world and tried to make it our own. As a whole, we are too prideful to admit that we are not in control because we want to dominate and take credit for something that's not ours or that we didn't do. We are supposed to be mere keepers of the world until Jesus comes back. Until we learn what love is, we will constantly have these problems because we focus on the negative and not the positive.

The word *love* is misused by many. I was guilty of that. I thought love was having fun, satisfying my appetites, and doing anything I wanted to do. But there's more to love than that. Love is an action verb; showing love involves making a choice. We have a world to think about, and the people in it. We show love by choosing to respect other people, even if we don't understand them.

We need to take a look at the root of the problem. As I researched it, I found out that in the United States 80 percent of crimes are done by males, and 20 percent of crimes are done by females. Men are under a lot of pressure to be leaders and take care of things. It used to be that most of them were brave, strong, and dominating. Only the men were allowed to work. Today the feminist movement has changed the workforce until is almost half female. Another fallout from the feminist movement is that men are being robbed of their masculine nature and taught to be sensitive and many times let the females dominate. That's why it is very important to train up our boys to become men. The best way to accomplish that is for the home to have both a father and a mother, but that's not happening these days, and this is hurtful to society.

Whether this generation wants to admit it or not, men are totally different from women in nature. For example, men like to hang together and play football, basketball, soccer, or video games, or attend sports events. It's called male bonding. You don't see a bunch of women outside playing games. So when a boy is not getting parental love at home, he goes to the streets with the other boys.

The single mother is busy taking care of the home and working one or two jobs, trying to support her children, and her boys spend too much time on their own. After they take care of their responsibilities, like taking out the trash, cutting the grass, or straightening their room, then they have extra time on their hands. They go outside and see cars riding up and down the street. They wish they had the money to get a car and take a girl joyriding. Before you know it, they get together with other boys, and start making plans to do wrong. It's called organized crime. Sadly, the boys involved in crime are getting younger and younger. We must pay more attention to our boys. If we don't, they are going to get in a lot of trouble before they're full grown. Men are more likely to commit crimes like robbery, murder, rape, or sexual assault according to "Crimes Women Are More Likely Than Men to Commit" by Sarah Kaufman (vocative.com, 6/17/2015).

Girls are not wired like men. Girls usually watch television, play with dolls, cook, or spend time on social media. Most girls just want a husband so they can be loved, have a family, and not have to deal with the bad guys on the streets. As already stated, women are responsible for approximately 20 percent of the crime in the US. Sarah Kaufman found that women are more likely to be locked up for crimes like larceny or theft, fraud, and drug possession. And although it's no longer considered a crime, many young women also have their unborn babies killed.

How does this happen? Remember your children are like a blank tape and, believe it or not, the home is where most of the problems start. Children know nothing as infants, but they learn quickly by watching what their parents are saying and doing. If you teach your child evil, they will be evil. If you teach them to be lazy, they will be lazy. If you teach them to cheat and lie, they will be cheaters and liars. So stop blaming others for deep-rooted problems that began in the home and then spread into the general public. As parents, you must build good relationships with your children so they feel comfortable talking to you about anything. And when your child is trying to talk to you, listen!

I taught my son how to cook and clean, so if he gets a wife it's because he wants one, not because he needs one. I want him to marry because he loves her. I taught my son to buy a small house before he gets married and take sole responsibility for paying the mortgage and maintaining the home. When he gets married and has children, he can get a larger home for his family, but keep the smaller home and rent it out. Then if things go wrong in his marriage, he will always have somewhere to go. If everything goes right, he will have extra income from the rental home to help with his growing family. I trained my son up on biblical principles; he listened to my instruction, and he listened to God. I refuse to let my son go through the kind of life experiences I had. I didn't want him to point at me someday and say I taught him the wrong things. To me, that's real love from mother to son. He now has that small house and two vehicles, and he's looking to find a wife, settle down, and raise a family. He is awesome!

There are too many divorces in this world simply because people don't know how to build good relationships; consequently, they're getting married for the wrong reasons. No matter how much money they have or how dominating they are, they can't make people love them. They don't understand that relationships are a lot of work, and sometimes they will get hurt. I want you to know that a relationship is like a covenant that two people agree to, and they vow to keep their commitments. That's why it's necessary to be truthful about what you expect out of a relationship. Relationships are complicated, and sometimes we have to have uncomfortable conversation to keep the relationship intact. We must find people we trust to hold us accountable for our actions. We make a choice to love and honor each other. Building strong families will build a strong, healthy society.

We've got to stop blaming everything on the White Man because he is only part of the problem. Humanity has had relationship problems since the beginning when Cain killed his brother Abel. We have to stop destroying our relationships and start communicating and building loving relationships, because, after all, love wins. Do you want to know how to build a healthy, loving relationship? Read I Corinthians 13. Here is part of it: "Love is patient and kind; love does not envy or boast; it is not arrogant or rude. It does not insist on its own way; it is not irritable or resentful; it does not rejoice at wrongdoing, but rejoices with the truth. Love bears all things, believes all things, hopes all things, endures all things. Love never ends. . . . now faith, hope, and love abide, these three; but the greatest of these is love."

I love you and want to you to be the best you can be. To that end, I have included an instruction guide that will help you learn how to get a loving and productive life and get a relationship with your Creator. I hope you realize that we all need help. I pray that we will all work together to become the people God wants us to be.

HOW TO HAVE A LOVING AND PRODUCTIVE LIFE BY MARILYN DAVIS

Introduction

In between love, happiness, heartache, and joy, I have learned one thing: most everybody wants to be loving and productive, but many people do not know how to go about it. After counseling and talking to many people with the same desire, I was asked to share with the public what I have discovered about how to become and how to create loving and productive people.

Since the age of eleven I have been interested in studying people from all walks of life and different socioeconomic levels. In my heart, I wanted to see everyone happy. However, life has shown me that will not happen because people are so diverse, each having a unique mindset and plan of action, whether good or bad. This can be discovered simply by watching episodes of true crime stories such as *American Greed*, *Cops*, and *Forensic Files*.

This complex world is filled with so many types of people that the human brain has difficulty comprehending the ways of man. God is the only One in the universe who understands all human motives, thoughts, words, and actions (Psa. 139:1–6).

So let's get started with how to become loving and productive.

How the Devil Got In

A lot of people ask, "Where is God?" or "Why does God seem so far away?" We see in I Samuel that the Israelites went against the prophet's advice, rejected God, and demanded a government similar to the surrounding nations (I Sam. 8:7–20). Similarly, our society has rejected God, banning Him from schools, courthouses, and other public places. We must realize we are in spiritual warfare and cannot win this battle through human ingenuity or strength. We need God's help to win the battle against Satan, the leader of the evil spiritual forces, for he is constantly roving about like a lion seeking human souls to devour (I Peter 5:8)!

How to Establish a Relationship with God

How does one become loving and productive? Think about this scenario: When you see a person in need on the street, what is your first inclination? Would you embrace them and take them into your home? Most would not. Instead, you probably would give them something to eat or a few dollars, pray for them, and send them off. The only way to develop a relationship with them would be to bring them into your home and allow them to stay. Relationship with God develop the same way. We need to invite Him in and spend time with Him. Although He knows our thoughts and actions (Psa. 139:1–6), He leaves it up to us to seek a relationship with Him. Once the relationship is established, then you're on the way to loving and productive living.

In developing a relationship with God, we accept certain truths as absolute:

1. The Word was with God in the beginning and came to life and dwelt on the Earth (John 1:1, 14).
2. If you confess that Jesus is Lord and believe He died and rose on the third day, you will be saved (Rom. 10:9–12).
3. Jesus is Lord. Repent and be baptized for the forgiveness of your sins (Acts 2:36, 38).
4. After taking these initial steps, we must "abide" in Christ in order to be productive (John 15:5–8).

After accepting Jesus Christ as Lord, we must do the following things daily to maintain a relationship with God:

1. Repent: Acts 2:36, 38
2. Pray: Phil. 4:4–7
3. Read the Word: Psa. 119:11
4. Apply the Word: James 1:23–25

Everyone Has Defects

Now that you are depending upon God, let us turn our attention to character defects. We all have them, but God loves us in spite of them. We view ourselves one way, but God sees us in a whole different way. Man looks on the outward appearance, but God looks on the heart (I Sam. 16:7). If we allow Him to, God is able to transform us into the people He created us to be. He created each of us for a specific purpose (I Cor. 12:12–27); whether or not we fulfill it is up to us. Either we will fulfill God's purpose for us by following His biblical instructions for our lives, or we will reject God's purpose for our lives by doing our own thing.

Giving God control of your life gives you access to His power and guidance. This brings adventure and intrigue, and you will never be bored! There will be no reason to be jealous, envious, mean, hateful, or cruel. You can stay busy and concentrate on fulfilling God's purpose for your life. However, if you do not surrender to God, you will develop an idle mind that will cause you to do and say things you will later regret.

Yes, everyone has defects. I've heard about them time and again. From working with people, I have learned that they tend to disclose TMI (Too Much Information). This could be taken two different ways: On the one hand, TMI could cause us to shut down a person who thought they could trust us more than anyone else. They would be disappointed and disillusioned. On the other hand, stopping them from talking before they are done can cause them to withdraw and thus never get the help they need. If you continue to stop people from talking to you, you will risk getting sugar-coated fabrications, which are useless. I would suggest that if you are unable to handle the subject matter they are speaking about, direct them to someone who can help them.

All of us have problems—both the people who are helping others and the people who are seeking help. We must humble ourselves. Also, when we are helping someone, our life story is what we are most likely to share. We may not have experienced everything, but we all have something to share.

Be careful not to judge another person for their decisions or opinions. Everyone has them: "I think this should be done this way," or "I think that should be done that way." Even if you know they are making the wrong choice, it is their choice! They will have to live with it. However, it is your responsibility to lovingly warn them when they are choosing the wrong path. God told Ezekiel he was like a watchman. If he saw the people making the wrong choice and doing the wrong thing and did not warn them, God would hold him responsible. But if he warned them and they did it anyway, Ezekiel would not be held responsible. All you can do in that case is to continue to love and pray for them. (See Ezek. 33.)

Children Need Training

Let's turn our attention to the children. Most people believe times have changed, but I say they have not. As a matter of fact, King Solomon in all his wisdom wrote that there was nothing new under the sun. In other words, down through the ages people just keep doing the same thing over and over (Eccl. 1:9).

It is my belief that our main disagreement with God is the way we raise our children. But I doubt today's issues will be solved unless we train up our children in the way they should go. This directive to parents is found in Proverbs 22:6. Children are born untrained and self-centered. Their only inborn ability is the know-how to get you to do what they want. Over time this can develop into negative and selfish emotions such as tantrums, fights, and public embarrassment. This behavior contributes to them becoming lazy, unproductive, irresponsible, out of control, and complaining about people of authority in their lives. They are neither loving nor productive. (See Paul's instruction in II Thess. 3:10.)

Therefore, I've compiled a shortlist of some important precepts that must be taught to children from the time they are small:

- Respect
- Patience (Prayer)
- Obedience (Forgiveness)
- Kindness
- Submission (Sitting/Being Still)
- Getting along with others

Here is what they must be taught during their teenage years so they can be productive in adult life:

- Chores
- Plans
- Bills
- Value of money
- How to shop (spouse, car, clothes, house, etc.)

One vital piece of advice is to always pray before you discipline, correct, or punish a child. After all, God knows them better than you (Psa. 139:1–6). Thank God He is fair and loves us very much. We are His children.

He blesses us, but to build our character, He also punishes us when we do wrong. We should raise our children in the same way. The Bible can guide us how to correct and build our children's character.

I guess my question to you is, "What are you producing out of your household?" If we are not loving and productive, then our children won't be loving and productive, and the world will not be helped. Given that you want your children to be fruitful and multiply, what kind of people are they when they leave the home? If more children were well taught and well trained, many more of the world's problems could be solved. Children would love God, love people, and be productive and useful.

Note: In this section about children I am not referring to the mentally challenged, the disabled, or the mentally ill. Despite their problems, some of them are loving and productive as well.

We Need Supernatural Help

If you maintain a good relationship with God, you will have peace that passes all understanding in every area of your life regardless of what happens (Phil. 4:7). Sure, you will have some heartache. People will do you wrong. But if you have a close relationship with God, you will be all right over time.

Now I know that might sound too good to be true, so let's discuss how difficult life can be. From childhood and up, I have heard and seen many stories of spousal and child abuse. It is an unfortunate truth that corruption happens at home. I know a case where the first real kiss a girl received was from her daddy. When she was nine years old, he kissed her and touched her inappropriately. When the girl told her mother what happened, the mother told her daughter not to start trouble in the family. Things like this happen all too often because of the lack of a foundation in Jesus Christ. It is very important to discuss abuse avoidance with your children as early as possible so they won't be vulnerable and unprotected.

God designed us to have freewill (Gen. 1:26), meaning we are free to choose to follow good or evil, right or wrong. We are born in sin into an imperfect world and are naturally selfish and self-serving (Psa. 51:5). Natural birth parallels spiritual birth. Spiritual birth is the most crucial step in having a loving and productive life. So how do you take this step? How do you acquire a foundation in Jesus Christ?

We must accept the absolute truth that we cannot win the battle against sin and the flesh without help. We need the help of supernatural forces to defeat sin and evil (Eph. 6:12–17). We cannot fight the battle based on feelings or emotions, which are deceitful (Jer. 17:9). We must hold each other accountable to recognize and correct our wrongdoing. A lot of gurus in the world are telling us to do this or do that. But the Bible is the instruction manual for how to live life successfully on Earth.

Adding Vibrancy to Your Relationship with God

Getting bored with the Bible is a sign that you have "settled on your lees" (Jer. 48:11), or gotten stuck in a rut in your comfort zone. But the Bible is a living, spiritual, never-ending book that can cut through all deception. When applied faithfully in your life, God's Word will have you falling in love with God. Maintaining a covenant relationship with Him will cause you to mature in the Lord; He will mold you and equip you to do the job He has assigned for you. I pray that everyone develops that kind of relationship with God, which not only will make you loving and productive, but it will be your eternal salvation.

Nevertheless, our selfish ways and "right now" attitudes stop us from wanting that kind of relationship with God because it takes a lot of work to develop. It involves more than sitting on a couch, waiting for God to do all the work.

We Need Each Other

Having peace in all circumstances requires a continuous pressing forward. At a young age I saw my father beating my mother, and I remember thinking to myself, "I don't ever want a man!" Remembering that, I have been told of many stories of abuse happening in the family and many of the people not getting proper help. This is why we need each other. We need to lead as many people as we can to repentance, prayer, Bible reading, obeying God, and applying the Word of God in their lives.

We Must Understand Both the Rich and the Needy

Young people think that being out of their parents' house and on their own means having freedom from rules. But if they do not have Jesus Christ as their foundation, they will only take the problems of their childhood out into the streets. Christian author and preacher Joyce Meyer famously said, "Hurting people hurt people." This goes for the rich as well as the poor, the needy and the greedy on every level. The rich think they need more money; some get it through legitimate means and others by dishonest means. Some rich people do right with the resources they have and some do wrong. Think of the stories of rich people who are depressed or who commit suicide. We must understand that money will not solve their issues. Fame and wealth will not bring peace and satisfaction.

We also have trouble seeing and understanding the poor around us (Matt. 26:11; Mark 14:7; Deut. 15:11). From my time of working in food pantries and outreaches to the poor, I have found that a majority of poor people are that way because of misfortune or mental illness. Many poor people lost their jobs when the company they worked for downsized or was taken over by another firm or simply shut down due to changes in technology. Some needy people will begin to do better with the support and free stuff they get and are healed from their temporarily disadvantaged status. Others will just continue to look for more to consume.

Loving and productive people will not add to this pain and suffering; they will understand that the Father has put them in the right place at the right time to fulfill His mission to save people (I Tim. 2:3–5). They must be out in the world loving God and serving people, because people matter to God (Luke 15; 19:10).

We All Have a Job to Do

We are born with good and evil inside us (Psa. 51:5; Gen. 1:26). It is part of the human condition. Although the human brain is complex, it is impossible for anyone to figure out all the world's problems. The God who created us is the only One who knows all the problems of all the people in the world (Rom. 8:27, 28). He is the only One who can save us. Religion cannot save people from themselves.

If you think or believe that you can keep it together all of the time, you are sadly mistaken. For example, what do you do when someone cuts you off while driving in traffic? Lose it? Say a curse word? Blow your horn? Give the offender a rude gesture? There are around 7.8 billion people in the world. Approximately 70 percent of the global population is in the workforce. Career Planner.com alone offers a list of 1,388 careers, but that is only a few of the thousands of job types around the globe. Because they are human, all of these workers are flawed and many times make poor choices and do wrong things.

For example, someone has to govern the countries of the world, but someone else has to clean the toilets of the world. What would happen if the sanitation engineers stopped cleaning, the plumbers stop fixing pipes, or the pest control workers stopped spraying for bugs? What would be the result of no government, no police, no court system, and no penal institutions? Now you are starting to get the picture. Total chaos!

Wasting time complaining and pointing fingers at each other is exhaustive, unproductive, and pointless. Do not get me wrong; we need constructive criticism to help us grow and improve. We need to allow the Holy Spirit to produce fruit in our lives—love, joy, peace, patience, kindness, goodness, faithfulness, gentleness, and self-control (Gal. 5). Wow! I wish I could do that consistently week after week, but after continuous daily attempts, I often fail. I repent, pray, read my Bible, and apply it. Sometimes I may start the day with an A and end the day with an F. But I keep trying and keep pushing!

Why I Serve God

I serve God for many reasons, and one of them is I do not have to be envious of anyone else because God gave me a job no one else can do. Out of 7.8 billion people, God designed each person to play a distinctive role in life, and each role is important. How awesome is that? The Holy Spirit teaches us how to please God (John 15:26). God wants a relationship with each one of us (Isa. 43:4). Although we were designed for God's enjoyment, some of us choose not to be His children. Those who choose not to be God's children are Satan's children (I John 3:10), and Satan's children will not inherit eternal life with God.

Our Father is a forgiving father; He is not a spiritual super cop who sits high on His throne and enjoys condemning people to hell. Consider that there are 613 rules and laws in the Bible. If you read and study the Bible, you will see that God repeatedly gives us multiple chances to repent and do right. He knows that in our flesh we are incapable of following all His rules and laws consistently. This is where Jesus Christ comes into the equation (Rom. 3:10, 21–24). He is the only One who can empower us to conquer ourselves. God's laws are no longer written on tables of stone; instead, He engraves them on the "fleshy tables of [our] heart" (II Cor. 3:1–7). His laws then become our inner motivation to please Him and complete the task He has given to us.

How to Read the Bible

When you have children to raise, you are responsible for using discernment based on the Bible. With this in mind, I find it helpful to read through the Bible once a year because I get something different from it each time I read it. It is a never-ending source of spiritual understanding and illumination.

I cannot say what the Bible is for you, but I can tell you this: you cannot read the Bible with the attitude that says, "I will read it through once and will have gleaned everything from it that I need to know." Reading the Bible from cover to cover will help you to discover that life is the same over the generations; it is merely the "same script with a different cast." This should humble you and your response should be to read, repent, pray, and apply. Upon following this procedure, you will find yourself entering a covenant relationship with God and being led by the Holy Spirit to study different areas of the Bible. This will lead you to apply what you learn to your life, and will open up many opportunities to fulfill God's plan for your life. These experiences are never boring!

Many people believe that as a Christian you have an unfair playing field, but you don't. When working in Christ, you will find that going through difficulties will build and strengthen your character, causing you to grow and mature throughout your life. Before I got saved, I got tired of doing the same thing every day. But as a Christian, I am never bored serving God and loving people, because people matter to God.

Think about it: Everyone comes in contact with different people. When we leave home each day, we are going in different directions and will encounter different people. If we are loving and productive and have a Bible-based foundation, we can minister to them and affect their lives.

My Desire

It is important to stay focused. If you will focus on the right and the things you are capable of changing, you can become the beautiful person you were designed by God to be. However, focusing on the wrong and on things you can't possibly change is a waste of time. I am not saying we should be ignorant of the world around us, but if we get involved in it, we will lose focus on what is in front of us and around us—that is, people who need God.

I am proposing that we all repent, pray, read, and apply the biblical principles to see where it takes us. If we love God with all our heart, all our mind, and all our soul, and our neighbor as ourselves, we will have access to His promises (Matt. 22:37, 38). We were created to "love God and serve people because people matter to God." My desire is that we live better, feel better, and most of all, know better.

The Father's Love Letter

An intimate message from God to you:

My child, you may not know Me, but I know everything about you.
I knew you even before you were conceived (Jer. 1:4–5).
I determined the exact time of your birth and where you would live (Acts 17:26).
You are fearfully and wonderfully made (Psa. 139:14).
I knitted you together in your mother's womb (Psa. 139:13) . . . and brought you forth on the day you were born (Psa. 71:6).
I know when you sit down and when you rise up. I am familiar with all your ways (Psa. 139:1–3).
Even the very hairs on your head are numbered (Matt. 10:29–31) . . . for you were made in My image (Gen. 1:27).
In Me you live and move and have your being, for you are My offspring (Acts 17:28).

I chose you when I planned creation (Eph. 1:11–12).

You were not a mistake, for all your days are written in My book (Psa. 139:15–16).

It is My desire to lavish My love on you simply because you are My child and I am your Father (I John 3:1).

I offer you more than your earthly father ever could (Matt. 7:11) . . . for I am the perfect Father (Matt. 5:48).

Every good gift that you receive comes from My hand (James 1:17) . . . for I am your provider and I meet all your needs (Matt. 6:31–33).

My plan for your future has always been filled with hope (Jer. 29:11) . . . because I love you with an everlasting love (Jer. 31:3).

My thoughts toward you are countless as the sand on the seashore (Psa. 139:17–18) . . . and I rejoice over you with singing (Zeph. 3:17).

I will never stop doing good to you (Jer. 32:40) . . . for you are My treasured possession (Exod. 19:5).

I desire to establish you with all My heart and all My soul (Jer. 32:41) . . . and I want to show you great and marvelous things (Jer. 33:3).

If you seek Me with all your heart, you will find Me (Deut. 4:29).

Delight in Me and I will give you the desires of your heart (Psa. 37:4) . . . for it is I who gave you those desires (Phil. 2:13).

I am able to do more for you than you could possibly imagine (Eph. 3:20) . . . for I am your greatest encourager (II Thess. 2:16–17).

I am also the Father who comforts you in all your troubles (II Cor. 1:3–4).

When you are brokenhearted, I am close to you (Psa. 34:18).

As a shepherd carries a lamb, I have carried you close to My heart (Isa. 40:11).

One day I will wipe away every tear from your eyes, and take away all the pain you have suffered on this earth (Rev. 21:3–4).

I am your Father, and I love you even as I love my son, Jesus (John 17:23) . . . for in Jesus, My love for you is revealed (John 17:26).

He is the exact representation of My being (Heb. 1:3).

He came to demonstrate that I am for you, not against you (Rom. 8:31) . . . and to tell you that I am not counting your sins against you (II Cor. 5:18–19).

Jesus died so that you could be reconciled to Me (II Cor. 5:18–19).

His death was the ultimate expression of My love for you (I John 4:10).

I gave up everything I loved that I might gain your love (Rom. 8:31–32).

If you receive the gift of My Son, Jesus, you receive Me (I John 2:23) . . . and nothing will ever separate you from My love again (Rom. 8:38–39).

Come home and I'll throw the biggest party heaven has ever seen (Luke 15:7).

I have always been Father, and will always be Father (Eph. 3:14–15).

My question is, Will you be my child? (John 1:12–13).

I am waiting for you (Luke 15:11–32).

Adapted from Father Heart Communications (1999)—FathersLoveLetter.com. Please feel free to copy and share with others.